TRAPPED IN THE PRINCIPAL'S OFFICE

Want more books by Debbie Dadey?

Swamp Monster in Third Grade

Swamp Monster in Third Grade #2:
Lizards in the Lunch Line

The Slime Wars

Slime Time!

The Worst Name in Third Grade

And don't forget to check out...

**Ghostville
Elementary**®

BY DEBBIE DADEY AND MARCIA THORNTON JONES

TRAPPED IN THE PRINCIPAL'S OFFICE

BY DEBBIE DADEY
ILLUSTRATIONS BY MARGEAUX LUCAS

A
LITTLE APPLE
PAPERBACK

SCHOLASTIC INC.

NEW YORK   TORONTO   LONDON   AUCKLAND   SYDNEY
MEXICO CITY   NEW DELHI   HONG KONG   BUENOS AIRES

To Maddy Lancaster, who suggested the title —D.D.

No part of this publication may be reproduced, stored in a retrieval system, or transmitted in any form or by any means, electronic, mechanical, photocopying, recording, or otherwise, without written permission of the publisher. For information regarding permission, write to Scholastic Inc., Attention: Permissions Department, 557 Broadway, New York, NY 10012.

ISBN 0-439-79400-5

12 11 10 9 8 7 6 5 4 3 2 1   5 6 7 8 9 10/0

Printed in the U.S.A.   40
First printing, November 2005

CONTENTS

1

Emily

A strange sound made Jake lift his green head up out of the murky water and listen. His swamp-monster hearing was especially good, and his memory was even better. He knew exactly who was making that sound. But why?

He had to find out, even though it was risky. Jake stopped hunting crawfish and swam away from his home in the darkest part of the swamp. He headed toward the most dangerous place in the world — the place where the humans were.

Jake swam as only a swamp monster

could, slicing through the slimy water like a speedboat. He didn't slow down until he reached the water's edge. "Emily?" he called.

No one else was around, so Jake quietly rose out of the swamp and padded toward the noisy figure. He couldn't live out of the water for long, but he had to see what was wrong. A girl was hunched over on a peeling wooden bench. Her black hair hung down and covered her face, but Jake was sure it was his old friend. His green skin tingled in the cool air. "Emily?" he said again, softly this time.

Emily looked up into the face of a monster. Slime dripped from the green spikes on the creature's head. Two horrid yellow eyes stuck out from its face. But it was the huge orange teeth that made Emily scream, "Help!"

Before Emily could do anything else, Jake put a hand on her shoulder. "Emily, don't you remember me? It's Jake."

"Jake?" Emily said, looking more closely at the dripping creature in front of her. "Is that really you?" Emily had seen Jake briefly as a swamp monster before, but it was still shocking to see him suddenly before her.

Jake nodded and sat down on the bench beside his friend. He had come to know Emily and her friends when he had accidentally turned himself into a human. Something about being near Emily again made his heart pound. "Why was water leaking from your eyes?" he asked.

Emily smiled and wiped the tears from her face. "I was crying because our principal thinks I drew pictures on the hallway walls."

4

Jake shuddered, and it wasn't because of the cool breeze. A swamp monster would never think of drawing on public property without permission. "Did you?" he asked.

"No," Emily snapped. "I brought the same kind of chalk to school that day for art class, so the principal thinks I'm guilty. But I'm going to find out who really did it, even if it takes me until the end of third grade."

"I'll help you," Jake told Emily.

"What can you do?" she asked.

Jake shrugged. "I can't do anything as a swamp monster. I'll have to become human again."

Emily shook her head firmly. "No, it's too dangerous. Swamp monsters need to be in the water."

Jake didn't say a word, but he knew he'd risk anything to help his friend.

2

Carrots

"You have to give them to me," Jake told his sister. They were in the swamp, hidden under the roots of a mangrove tree. The cool water lapped at their waists.

Nancy snatched a mosquito out of the air and popped it into her mouth. Then she looked at Jake and shook her head. Swamp water flew out of her stringy blond hair. "I don't *have* to give you anything. I found those carrots, fair and square."

It was true. Nancy had grabbed a whole bag of carrots when Jake had thrown them into the swamp. She'd found them,

so they were hers. That was the swamp-monster way.

"But carrots are the only thing that will make me human again. I *have* to help Emily," Jake explained.

Nancy rolled her yellow eyes. "Why would you want to help one of those web-less creatures? Humans don't even have gills. It's not normal."

"Emily helped me when I needed it," Jake explained. "I can't turn away from her now." Jake had found a carrot near the swamp. Surprisingly, eating it had turned him human. Emily had been the one who had helped him back into the swamp when the carrot had worn off and he'd turned back into a swamp monster on dry land. Jake shuddered thinking about what could have happened to him without Emily's help. He wasn't sure how he could help her, but he had to try.

Nancy sighed and pulled a soggy plastic bag out of her backpack. She grabbed a handful of carrots from the bag. The swamp water had preserved them pretty well. The carrots were a little brown, but mostly orange.

"Don't you dare tell Mom and Dad I gave you these," Nancy said. "I'd be in trouble until I was old enough to go deep-swamp diving."

Jake grinned and nodded his fin-covered head. "Thanks, Nancy. I owe you for this."

Nancy smiled. "I know, and don't you forget it. Someday you'll have to pay me back."

"I know, I know," Jake said. "Cover for me while I'm gone? Tell them I'm visiting a friend." Jake gave his sister a hug, grabbed the carrots, and swam quickly through the murky swamp water.

By the time Jake came out on dry land, the sky was turning black. Green goose bumps popped out on Jake's scaly skin as he stepped into the cool evening air. But Jake didn't worry about that. Instead, he looked around for Emily. She was nowhere to be seen. Jake's keen swamp-monster hearing didn't help, either. There was no one around, except for an owl hooting miles away.

"How in the world am I going to find Emily again?" Jake wondered out loud. He figured that becoming a human was a step in the right direction. He took a deep breath, opened his mouth, and ate the carrots Nancy had given him.

After that, everything went black.

3

Swamp-Monster Snack

Jake rolled over in the soft, squishy mud. The mud felt great, but something was wrong. Jake sat up straight. He wasn't in the swamp. And he was *human*!

Jake shook his head. Ouch! His stomach hurt and his eyes felt funny. He'd forgotten how hard it was to turn human. He tried to stand up, but the trees swirled around him and he felt like throwing up the frogs he'd eaten for lunch.

"Steady," Jake told himself. "You can't help Emily if you're sick." He really wanted to figure out who had made the mess at Emily's school, but first he had to find her.

Jake had been to Emily's house once before, but he didn't know if he could find the way by himself, especially since the evening sky grew darker by the minute.

Jake took one step, then another. Finally, his legs were land-worthy. "I think it's this way," he said out loud. He pushed through some bushes and found himself on a side-walk. The concrete hurt his bare feet. Why would humans walk on something that was so hard?

Luckily, Jake had brought along the pants he'd gotten the last time he'd turned human. He knew that the people on dry land would have a fit if they found him naked. Webless creatures sure had some strange ideas about being comfortable. Swamp monsters didn't ever have to worry about clothes.

Jake stopped in the middle of the side-walk. He'd come to a group of houses, but something wasn't right. He'd never been here before. Jake had a great memory. Why hadn't he paid more attention the last time he'd been to Emily's house?

Jake turned in circles. He wasn't sure which way he'd come. Everything looked the same. At least in the swamp, the trees looked different. "Oh, great," he said to himself. "Now I've gotten myself lost in human territory. What else can go wrong?"

A deep growl answered him. A big, black dog stepped out from behind a trash can and bared its teeth. Jake had seen dogs before, but never one that growled like this Doberman pinscher.

"Nice dog," Jake said softly.

This dog wasn't nice at all. In fact, this dog looked like it wanted a swamp monster for a snack. Jake backed away. The dog hunched down low, like it was going to attack.

Jake gulped. He'd never be able to help Emily now. His parents would never know what happened to him. No one except the dog would know. Jake had a feeling the dog wouldn't be telling anyone anything.

The dog leaped into the air and Jake closed his eyes, preparing for the worst. Then he felt something grab his shoulder.

4

Killer

"Aaaaaaahhhhh!" screamed Jake.

"Stop!" cried a familiar voice.

"Nancy?" Jake said. "What are you doing here?"

"Saving your fins," she answered. She pointed a pale finger at the huge black dog. It whined and rolled belly-up on the ground. Animals always seemed to listen to Nancy. Even swamp alligators did what Nancy wanted them to do. Jake's uncle Leonard thought that Nancy had a gift.

Jake looked closely at Nancy and got the shock of his life. "You're not green!" he shrieked.

"No kidding," she said. "I figured it was *my* turn to be human."

Jake shook his head in disbelief. Nancy's blond hair hung in messy strands around her human face. Gone were her green webs and fins. Gone were the pointy spines on her back. Instead, she was dressed in a too-big shirt that Jake had stashed in his cave.

"I thought you were going to help your friend Emily," Nancy said.

Jake shrugged, embarrassed. "I'm not sure how to get to her house."

Nancy rolled her big yellow eyes and bent down to whisper in the dog's ear. "Don't get too close to that animal," Jake warned. "He's a killer."

The big dog licked Nancy's cheek and whined. "Some killer," Nancy said with a chuckle. "He'll show us the way to Emily's house."

The dog trotted off and Jake shook his head. "That dog is going to take us to meet some of his mangy friends. They'll probably eat us for a late-night snack."

But Nancy didn't listen to her brother. She followed the dog. Jake didn't have much of a choice, so he took off after Nancy. They ended up right outside Emily's house. The dog barked and Emily came to the window.

"Jake!" Emily squealed. "You're human again!"

"I'm here to help solve your mystery," Jake explained. His face turned a little bit red.

"Hi," Nancy added. "I'm Jake's sister, Nancy. I'm here to keep him from being eaten by vicious animals." The big Doberman pinscher barked, licked Nancy's hand, and trotted away to its home.

Emily opened her window and the two swamp monsters crawled inside. Nancy's big eyes got even bigger when she looked around Emily's room. It had a bed, a chair, and a dresser. Posters of cute, fluffy dogs hung on the walls. "This is the weirdest place I've ever seen," Nancy muttered.

Emily shrugged. "Most humans have rooms sort of like this. Why don't you sleep in my brother's room tonight? He's away at college and he has bunk beds." Jake and Nancy looked at each other quizzically.

Emily led them down the hall and pointed at a huge wooden and cloth contraption. "You can sleep there."

Nancy shook her head in disgust at the white pillows and blue bedspreads. "There's no way I could lie down on a thing like that. It's not natural."

Jake sighed. He had a feeling Nancy wasn't

going to like being a webless creature one bit.

"What's in there?" Nancy asked, pointing to a little room off of the bedroom.

"That's my brother's bathroom," Emily explained. "You can get a drink of water there, if you're thirsty."

"Water?" Nancy said with a smile. Ten minutes later, Nancy was up to her neck in warm water, sound asleep in the bathtub.

Emily giggled as she said goodnight to Jake. "My brother will never believe that a swamp monster was in his bathtub."

Jake couldn't believe it, either. He just wondered what would happen tomorrow.

5

Go, Nancy

"That's my school." Emily pointed to a tall brick building. Ivy grew up the side and a huge rack of metal objects with wheels sat near the door. Kids ran all over the school yard, throwing balls back and forth and racing one another.

"Whoa!" Jake yelped when a boy on one of the wheeled metal contraptions almost rolled into him.

Emily pulled Jake and Nancy out of the way. "Don't worry," she said. "That's just a bicycle. We ride them sometimes."

Nancy grinned. "I'd like to try that."

"Sure," Emily said. "How about after school?"

But Nancy never liked to wait for things. "Hi," she said to the boy on the bike. "I'm Nancy."

"Hi," the boy said with a shrug.

"I've never ridden one of those before. Can I try yours?"

The boy looked at her in disbelief. "You've never ridden a bike? Are you from Mars?"

This time Nancy shrugged. "They don't have bikes where I'm from."

The boy helped Nancy onto the bike and even held on to the handlebars for her. He walked alongside her and held the bike as she wobbled.

"Hey, Victor," another kid yelled at the boy. "What are you doing?"

"I'm teaching Nancy how to ride a bike," Victor admitted. "She's new here."

A group of girls saw Nancy wobbling and yelled, "Go, Nancy. You can do it!"

Pretty soon a huge group was cheering for Nancy. In just a minute, it seemed like everyone on the playground had stopped to watch her. "Go, Nancy. Go, Nancy!" they chanted.

Just then, Victor let go of the handlebars and Nancy rode off on the bike by herself. Jake's heart swelled with pride for his little sister. She wasn't afraid of anything! Well, almost anything.

Nancy coasted to a stop, hopped off the bike, and shook Victor's hand. In fact, she went around the big crowd of kids and shook as many hands as she could. "Hi, I'm Nancy. I'm new here," she said. "Let's play sometime."

Jake smiled. Leave it to Nancy to make friends with everyone at Glenstone

Elementary before the school day even started. That was just like her. Suddenly, as he watched his sister, Jake stopped smiling. Nancy's face was turning swamp-monster green!

6

Swamp Monster on the Wall

Jake grabbed his little sister's arm and tried to pull her away from the playground. "We have to get you out of here right now!" he cried.

Nancy frowned. "I'm having fun. Look at all my new friends." A big group of girls stood around Nancy, smiling and laughing. Thankfully, none of them noticed the green glow on Nancy's face.

Jake leaned over to whisper in Nancy's ear. "You're also turning green. Let's get back to the swamp before something awful happens."

"No problem," Nancy said, pulling the bag of carrots from the pocket of the pants Emily had lent her. She chewed up a few and gave the last two carrots to Jake.

"Is this all we have left?" Jake asked. "I think we'd better leave."

Nancy shook her head as the bell rang. "This place is too exciting. I can't wait to see more!"

As the big crowd of kids headed inside the school, everyone fell silent. A big picture of what looked like a swamp monster had been scribbled on the wall in brightly colored chalk.

Emily gasped. "Who would do something so awful?"

Jake shook his head. A swamp monster would never destroy his environment. "It does look a little like our cousin

Dominick," Jake whispered to Nancy. Dominick had turned human once and caused all kinds of trouble at Glenstone Elementary.

The big crowd of students parted as Principal Pellman stormed down the hall. "Did you do this?" she asked, glaring at Emily.

"No," Emily said, her lip quivering. "I just got here. Ask Jake."

Principal Pellman glared at Jake. He gulped and wondered if she'd let him visit the school again, but Principal Pellman was too upset about the wall to notice Jake. "This sort of behavior will not be tolerated at Glenstone Elementary," she said. "I will catch whoever did this, and that student will be very sorry."

Emily looked like she was ready to cry. She walked silently into the classroom and put her head on her desk. Jake patted her shoulder. "Don't worry, Emily. We'll find out who drew on the wall."

Emily sniffed. "The principal thinks I did it, but I didn't. I promise!"

"Sure," snapped the class bully, Ted, as he walked by Emily's desk. "I bet little

Miss Goody Two-shoes did it yesterday after school."

Jake wanted to yell at Ted. Jake wanted to wrestle him to the ground, but humans didn't do things like that at school. Jake knew that . . . but Nancy didn't.

7

Wrestling

Nancy leaped on Ted. They fell to the floor and rolled. Nancy had wrestled plenty of alligators and snakes in the swamp, but Jake couldn't believe she was wrestling the school bully. Ted stood at least a foot taller than Nancy, but that didn't slow her down one bit.

"Stop!" Jake cried. It took Emily, Jake, and a boy named Tommy to pull Nancy off of Ted.

"That girl is crazy!" Ted yelled.

Nancy folded her arms over her chest. "I'm not crazy. I just don't like it when you're mean to my friend."

Emily couldn't help smiling at Nancy. Emily didn't believe in fighting, but she had never met a girl quite like Nancy.

Jake pulled Nancy to the back of the room. Luckily, Emily's teacher wasn't in the classroom yet. There was still time for the swamp monsters to leave. "This is a human school," Jake explained. "People don't wrestle when they have to solve a problem. They talk about it."

"Why do they do that?" Nancy asked. "Wrestling is so much faster."

"But somebody might get hurt," Jake said.

Nancy pumped her arm in the air to show her muscles. "Not me! I'm strong."

"I really think we should go back to the swamp now," Jake told her.

"But what about the mystery?" Nancy

asked. "We can't leave without helping Emily. That's what we came to do, remember?"

Jake nodded, but he didn't know what to do about Nancy. How could he explain his little sister to Emily's teacher? And what if Nancy started another fight?

While Jake was deep in thought, Nancy disappeared. Jake shook his head and looked around. Kids all over the room were finding their seats and putting their books away. But Nancy was nowhere to be seen.

"Tommy," Jake whispered. "Did you see where Nancy went?"

Tommy pointed toward the hallway. "I think she went out there. Maybe she went to the bathroom."

Jake nodded. "Tell Emily I'll see her later."

He ran out into the hall just in time to

see Nancy's blond head disappear into the cafeteria. "Wait!" he yelled.

Jake chased after his sister. As he rounded the corner into the cafeteria, he couldn't believe what he saw.

8

Pudding

"Stop!" Jake yelled. Had Nancy gone crazy? She was pouring huge tubs of butterscotch pudding onto the cafeteria floor.

Nancy smiled at her brother. "This stuff is even better than mud. Watch this!"

Nancy took a running start and slid through the mess on the floor. Pudding splattered behind her in a brown spray. Nancy fell on her rear and kept on sliding. "Wheeeeee!" she screamed.

She slid right into a small table that held ketchup, mustard, and pickles. The table toppled and everything landed on Nancy's head. She stood up, covered in red, yellow, green, and brown gook.

"You look like the inside of the trash can down by the swamp," Jake said.

Nancy laughed. "I thought webless creatures were weird, but they definitely know how to have fun."

Jake shook his head. "Humans do *not* do this for fun. In fact, we'd better get this cleaned up — fast."

"No way," Nancy said. "I want to play some more."

Jake knew how hard it was to get Nancy to stop fooling around, so he said, "You stay right here. I'll find something to clean up this mess with before we both get in big trouble."

Jake walked back into the kitchen and found a huge roll of paper towels, a mop, and a bucket. "This should do the trick," he said.

Jake walked out of the kitchen just in time to see Principal Pellman leading a very pudding-covered Nancy out of the cafeteria. The door closed with a thud behind them. "Oh, no," he whispered. "*Now* what am I going to do?"

Jake rushed across the cafeteria after Nancy. Unfortunately, he forgot about the pudding. He stepped into the spill and slid. "Awwwww!" He sped across the floor on his rear end. The bucket, towels, and mop flew up in the air. Jake landed with a thud against the ketchup table.

Splat! Ketchup hit him in the chin.

Splat! Mustard hit him in the nose.

Splat! Two pickles hit him in the eyes.

Jake groaned. Could things get any worse?

Bam! The bucket landed on his foot.

Bam! The paper towels landed on his lap.

Bam! The mop landed on his head.

9

Zoo Cage

Jake tossed the mop off his head and the paper towels off his lap. He kicked at the bucket, but it was stuck tight on his foot. He'd just have to leave it there for now. He had to help Nancy! Jake took off down the hall.

Slap. Plop. Slap. Plop. The bucket and his sneaker made strange sounds on the hallway floor. After a long walk, Jake reached the principal's office too late. The door was shut tight. A trail of pudding on the floor led inside.

A blob of mustard dribbled down Jake's neck and he wiped it away. A horrible

feeling filled his stomach, but he couldn't wipe that away. What if Nancy changed into a swamp monster in front of the principal? There was no telling what would happen!

Visions of Nancy in a zoo cage flashed through Jake's mind. Most humans had never seen a swamp monster before. Jake knew he had to do something, and fast. He could already feel a little slit on his neck. It wouldn't be long before a swamp-monster gill would form there.

Jake opened the door and walked into the outer office. He would grab Nancy, and they'd run back to the swamp as quickly as possible.

"Stop right there, young man," the secretary said, putting down a cup of coffee. "Principal Pellman is busy. You need to get back to class."

"But . . ." Jake said.

The secretary shook her head and stood in front of the principal's door. She pointed one long pink fingernail toward the hall-way. "Out!"

Jake lowered his head and slunk out of the office. The bucket clanged against the floor as he walked. Jake felt as gloomy as the bottom of the swamp, but he could see that the sun was shining in through a hall-way window.

A window! That was the answer. He'd sneak into the principal's office through a window and grab Nancy. Or maybe he could wave to her to climb out and escape.

Slap. Plop. Slap. Plop. Jake raced out of the school as fast as he could with the bucket on his foot. He ran around to the side of the building. "This has to be the right window," Jake said to himself.

Unfortunately, the window was so high that Jake couldn't see in. He looked around to find something to stand on. He didn't find a rock or a ladder, but he found something even better.

10

Blue Chalk

"So you're the one!" Jake yelled at Ted.

Ted stood nearby, looking surprised. He stopped drawing on the brick wall and stared at Jake. "What are you going to do about it?" Ted said with a sneer. "You can't stop me."

Jake clomped over to Ted. With the bucket still on his foot, Jake grabbed the chalk out of Ted's hand. "Why would you do something like this? Don't you know it's wrong?"

Ted wiped the blue chalk off his hands, onto the back of his pants. He shrugged. "I like to draw and paint, but I never get the

chance. I got kicked out of art class for bullying a classmate. Putrid Pellman is a mean old bat."

Jake's mouth dropped. He had figured Ted was drawing everywhere just to be mean. "You know," Jake said, "that swamp monster drawing was pretty good."

Ted grinned. "You think so?"

Jake nodded. "What did you draw here?"

"It's the swamp. Do you like it?" Ted asked.

Jake looked at the big tree Ted had drawn. Its branches dropped down over weeds and water. An old bench sat nearby. "It looks just like the swamp," Jake admitted.

"The swamp is pretty cool," Ted said.

"You should tell Principal Pellman that you love to draw," Jake suggested. "Maybe she'd let you back into art class."

"Are you kidding?" Ted said, raising his

voice. "Everyone would laugh at me." Ted grabbed Jake's shirt and put a fist to his nose. "If you tell anyone that I like art, I'll punch you into the swamp. Got it?"

Jake gulped. "Got it."

Suddenly the window above the two boys opened and Principal Pellman stuck out her head. "Who's yelling out there?"

Ted dived into the bushes, leaving Jake staring up at the principal.

"You!" snapped Principal Pellman.

"Uh-oh!" Jake said, looking at the blue chalk in his hand.

11

Caught Blue-Handed

Principal Pellman ran outside and grabbed Jake by the arm in no time flat.

"Uh-oh!" Jake said again, but this time it wasn't because he'd been caught with chalk in his hand. It was because his skin was turning green. Not only that, but Jake's sneakers felt squishy and his neck itched like crazy. His gills were popping out. Jake had to get away before it was too late. But what about Nancy? He couldn't just leave her trapped in the principal's office.

But Nancy didn't wait for his help. She jumped out of the window and landed in the bushes — right on top of Ted.

Ted stormed out of the bushes with Nancy on his shoulders. "Get off of me!" he shrieked.

"What is going on here?" Principal Pellman said. "Nancy, get off of him."

Jake pointed to Ted. "He's the one who's been drawing on everything! It's because he loves to draw and paint so much."

The principal shook her head. "But you're the one with the chalk in your hand."

"I took it away from Ted. He loves to draw," Jake told her. Jake hoped she would believe him, because Nancy's face was looking green, and her eyes were definitely turning bright yellow.

"Look at the back of his pants," Nancy suggested, pulling Ted's ear until he turned around.

Sure enough, the back of Ted's pants were covered with blue chalk where he'd

wiped his hands. "Ted!" Principal Pellman snapped. "Why didn't you tell me that you liked to draw?"

Nancy jumped down and Ted's face turned red. "I was embarrassed."

"Art is very important," Principal Pellman admitted. "I never should have banned you from that class. I'll let you go back."

"You will?" Ted said with a surprised look on his face.

"Of course," Principal Pellman said. "But you'll have to wash the walls."

Ted nodded.

"And I'll have to punish you for drawing on school property without permission," she added.

Ted frowned and clenched his fists.

"I have a suggestion," Jake said.

12

Smiling Monsters

One week later, Emily and Tommy stood by the swamp. "It looks great," Tommy admitted.

"Who would have ever thought that Ted could fix up the old bench and make it look so cool?" Emily said. "I don't know what made Principal Pellman suggest that he paint it, but it was a great idea."

The old bench's new paint job glistened in the sun. Emily especially liked what Ted had painted on the bench. Not one but two swamp monsters' faces were on the back of the bench, smiling at her.

Emily looked wistfully toward the

swamp. Jake and his sister had disappeared. Emily knew they had gone back to the swamp. At least, she hoped so. She knew that swamp monsters couldn't stay out of the swamp too long without getting ill. Emily definitely didn't want Jake to get sick.

"Do you think we'll ever see a real swamp monster again?" Tommy asked.

"It would be nice," Emily said.

"I bet they'd like this bench," Tommy said.

Emily nodded and walked away with Tommy, but she dropped something in the trash can as she left. A few minutes later, two slimy green creatures rose up out of the water. Looking around to make sure they were alone, they trodded toward the bench.

"The paintings look good," Jake said.

"No fair," Nancy said. "Why aren't there any girls?"

Jake shrugged. "I guess Ted has never seen a girl swamp monster before."

Nancy put her hands on her hips. "What are you talking about? A girl swamp monster wrestled with him and pulled his ear."

Jake laughed. "Yeah, but you were a human when you did it."

Nancy frowned and flicked a piece of weed off of her green arm. "Maybe I'll just have to show Ted exactly what a girl swamp monster looks like."

"Oh, no, you don't," Jake said. "Our human adventures are over, once and for all. Do you know how close you came to being put in a zoo cage?"

"Maybe you're right," Nancy said. "I guess we should leave dry land to the humans."

Jake splashed back into the swamp, thankful that his sister was back to her sensible self. What he didn't notice was that Nancy had taken something out of the trash can — a bag of carrots.